ARCHIE'S AMAZING GAME

Michael Hardcastle

Illustrated by Michael Reid

Hi! I'm Archie. Mum said I can't play footie, but I can't live without it...

A & C Black • London

comix

First paperback edition 2003
First published 2002 in hardback by
A & C Black Publishers Ltd
37 Soho Square, London W1D 3QZ
www.acblack.com

Text copyright © 2002 Michael Hardcastle
Illustrations copyright © 2002 Michael Reid

The rights of Michael Hardcastle and Michael Reid to be identified
as author and illustrator of this work have been asserted by them in
accordance with the Copyrights, Designs and Patents Act 1988.

ISBN 0-7136-6287-5

A CIP catalogue for this book is available from the
British Library.

A & C Black uses paper produced with elemental, chlorine-free pulp,
harvested from managed sustainable forests.

Printed and bound in Spain by G. Z. Printek, Bilbao

CHAPTER ONE

Kyle smiled. He could afford to, he wasn't the one with the problem.

Don't get yourself all hot and bothered. Just forget what your mum says.

Give her time. She'll give way before long, you'll see. Mums always do. Just wait a while, Arch.

Archie scratched his head and frowned at his best friend. He'd expected him to offer some really useful advice instead of recommending that he do nothing at all. Perhaps, though, Kyle didn't really understand how big a problem this ban on football was.

Kyle was moving gently on the park swing, his arms wrapped round the supporting chains, looking as if he were in a dream.

Look, I've got to be able to play football, you know that.

As if to prove it, he began bouncing the ball on his left instep. He kept that up for some moments before flicking it on to his right instep.

Then he sent it higher and caught it on the nape of his neck before allowing it to run down his sloping back to the ground.

It was an impressive trick Kyle had seen many times.

But Mum says I've got to pack it in for the whole week we're on this stupid holiday!

She says I've got to do what the doctor says and let my ankle recover from that stupid little injury. It has recovered, if you ask me.

You can see that I'm fine, so why can't she?

Oh yeah, and Mum also says if I have a break from football on holiday then my brother and sister will always be free to do what they want to do.

My dad says that when you desperately want something for yourself you should get everybody you can on your side so they can support you.

So that's it, you see — fix things so your mum's outnumbered. Okay?

Archie really liked the sound of that.

Kyle shrugged.

'Oh, girls,' muttered Archie dismissively as his best friend darted across the park at a striker's speed.

He normally moved fast himself but now he went home at a snail's pace. Archie's head filled with thoughts of how he might persuade his brother and sister to help him get what he wanted when the family went on holiday to Carnegie Parc next week. He couldn't come up with anything better, though, than Kyle's suggestion.

CHAPTER TWO

Archie's mum was lying on the sofa in the lounge, reading a book. It was a familiar sight because she loved reading. She believed that just about everything in life could be learned from a book.

She knew her oldest son had a quick temper at times.

'Maybe,' Archie answered, keen to keep her happy.

Where he usually is at this time on a Sunday, I imagine: fishing at Merridale.

'Thanks,' said Archie, departing at his usual speed. Merridale was hidden away at the bottom of the valley and it wouldn't take him long to get there. It would be a hard slog on the way back home but it would be worth it if he'd got what he wanted from Ross.

CHAPTER THREE

Caught anything?

Archie was very friendly when he saw his brother. Ross was the only person fishing on that part of the riverbank but Archie knew he liked his own company best of all.

Just missed a couple of big 'uns!

Ross looked gloomy.

Archie handed it over. Ross unwrapped it immediately and stuffed half of it into his mouth. He didn't take his eyes off his fishing rod, however, or the line in the water.

It's a deal, then?

Archie pressed him.

No, but I'll think about doing it for two bars a day.

Ross knew how to bargain.

Archie hesitated. That would cost him quite a lot of money. Still, he needed his brother on his side. His support was vital if he was to outwit his mum.

Then he produced his notebook, scribbled in it and handed it over to Ross with a pencil.

Ross sighed at his brother's strange ways, but tucked his rod under his arm and rather awkwardly put his signature on the page. Archie grinned. He knew his brother couldn't resist a bribe of chocolate.

CHAPTER FOUR

Minutes later Archie was puffing his way to the top of the hill, plotting how to get Jenny on his side too.

She liked football, she even trained sometimes with Archie, but she loved tennis. She was convinced she would win Wimbledon one day.

Somehow, he had to fix it so that she would agree to play in the mini-football tournament as well as the tennis tournament. This would be tricky because Tom, a boy at her school who was also coming with his family to Carnegie Parc, had agreed to be her partner at tennis.

Archie crept into the house trying not to disturb his mum. He went up to his room so he could work out a plan in peace.

After tea Archie took his notebook and set off at speed on his bike. Tom would be practising with Jenny and hopefully Archie would be able to catch him on his own. First, though, he knew he had to win them over by playing some tennis himself.

Jenny was amazed to see him but she was also delighted.

Archie hits the ball harder than anyone I know so he really makes me run around.

Then she giggled.

Trouble is, his shots can go anywhere! He's not accurate like you, partner.

Archie didn't contradict her but when they were all knocking up he tried to avoid making any wild shots. For his plan to work he needed them both to believe that he was really improving as a tennis player.

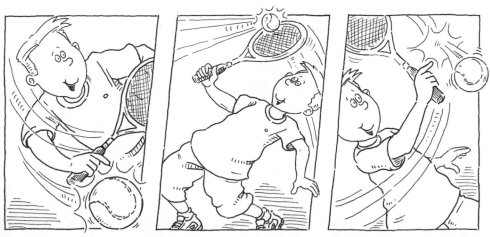

When it was time to finish, Jenny shook her long hair free and turned to her brother.

You know, Archie, you ought to play in the tournament at Carnegie. If you find a good partner you might even meet Tom and me in the final. Mind you, we'd thrash you out of sight!

Archie shook his head.

Once he and Tom were in the boys' changing room, however, he set his plan in action.

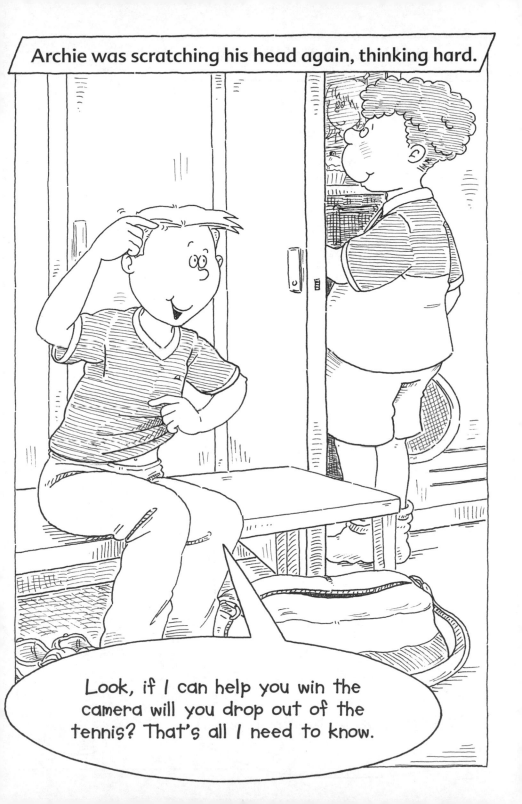

Tom did his own bit of thinking.

I suppose I might. But I don't really want to.

Very decisively, Archie stood up.

Right! I'll be in touch, Tom.

Tom just gave a sort of nod as Archie slid his notebook back into his pocket before striding off towards his bike. This wasn't the moment to talk to his sister about anything.

CHAPTER FIVE

The night before they were going on holiday Archie cycled round to Kyle's house and suggested they had some football practice.

It was only when the practice was finished that Archie raised the subject that had taken him to Kyle's.

His friend frowned.

Oh, I don't know. I mean, it was very expensive, so—

I'll look after it. You know me, I'm always careful.

Tell you what, I'll give you a new film when I return it. Two, if you like. That's like a fee, isn't it?

Kyle liked a bargain. He thought for a minute then agreed to Archie's deal.

Okay, then! And you've got my promise I'll take care of it.

Like a conjuror, Archie produced his notebook with a flourish.

I don't make just any old promise. I write things down in this book — and I'll sign it so you'll have proof if you need it.

While Kyle watched in surprise, Archie scribbled away and then added his signature. He held the page up to Kyle who read it and then nodded again.

Okay, Arch, I'll trust you. Hang on, I'll go and get it.

Archie rubbed his hands in glee. He'd pulled off another trick for his game plan.

CHAPTER SIX

As soon as the family was settled in their cabin at Carnegie Parc, Mum had something to say to them.

Ross was about to say something when Archie grabbed his arm to keep him quiet.

Not now, Ross. We'll show our united front later.

He still had to win Jenny over first.

He wasted no time in going to find Tom who was just about to go to the swimming pool, already dressed in his trunks. 'I've been thinking, I don't...' Tom said, when suddenly Archie produced the borrowed camera from behind his back.

Wow!

Tom's eyes were gleaming.

'Yes,' agreed Archie, pulling out his notebook.

'I don't know what Jenny's going to say...' Tom remarked sorrowfully as he autographed the page without even reading it.

'Course I am,' agreed Archie, trying not to look too pleased with himself.

Later that day Jenny came in from a practice session at the tennis courts and asked Archie if he knew where Tom was — he hadn't been at practice.

Archie nodded.

And Archie told her that he was willing to take Tom's place just so long as she agreed to take part in the football tournament.

He'd already been to see the organiser and suggested to him that girls should be allowed to play because some, like his sister, were mad keen on the game — and also brilliant players. The coach, impressed by Archie's obvious devotion to his sister, agreed immediately. He was going to put up special notices to attract more players.

Naturally, Archie didn't tell Jen all those details, he merely pulled out his notebook, opening it at a fresh page.

I'll sign this to say I'll be your tennis partner and then you can sign to say you agree to play football.

Ross wants to play soccer, too.

To his amazement, she simply beamed at him.

That's quite exciting about the football.
Are there any medals? I fancy winning one.

Archie thrust the notebook under her nose. 'Just sign,' he urged, in case she changed her mind.

CHAPTER SEVEN

That night he tried to decide when would be the best moment to tell Mum what he and Jenny and Ross wanted. She'd suspect he'd been plotting to get his own way. But the signatures in the notebook would prove football mattered to all of them.

He was just about asleep when Mum tapped on the door and came in.

Archie, I've been thinking. I realise I haven't been fair to you, banning your footie. You didn't complain once and you've also been really good helping Jenny with her tennis.

Several thoughts went through Archie's mind at once. He was stunned. All his clever planning had been for nothing! Mum had simply given in. Kyle had been right all along when he said mums changed their minds in time. Why hadn't he trusted Kyle's advice?

I'm glad you're pleased, darling. So have a good sleep and enjoy your first game tomorrow.

Archie collapsed on his pillow, still not knowing whether to be pleased or furious. He was getting his way after all. But at some cost. His mind began to click into gear again.

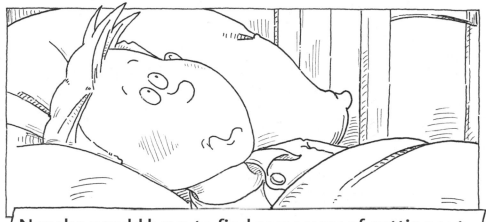

Now he would have to find some way of getting out of his promise to feed all that chocolate to his greedy brother.

But Archie remembered the notebook and the signed promise. He had been so sure the notebook was a clever idea.

Then his mind ticked over again. Archie smiled.

Mmm. There might be a way round this...